THE
DATE

THE DO-OVER

THE DATE FAIL

**BRENDA
SCOTT ROYCE**

darbycreek

MINNEAPOLIS

Darby Creek
A division of Lerner Publishing Group, Inc.
241 First Avenue North
Minneapolis, MN 55401 USA

For reading levels and more information, look up this title at www.lernerbooks.com.

Image credits: ND700/Shutterstock.com; VshenZ/Shutterstock.com.

Main body text set in Janson Text LT Std 12/17.5.
Typeface provided by Adobe Systems.

Library of Congress Cataloging-in-Publication Data

Names: Royce, Brenda Scott, author.
Title: The date / Brenda Scott Royce.
Description: Minneapolis : Darby Creek, [2019] | Series: The do-over | Summary:
    After a disastous attempt to ask her crush, Evan, on a date, Maribel finds herself
    stuck on the last day of school, trying over and over to get it right.
Identifiers: LCCN 2018027162 (print) | LCCN 2018034934 (ebook) |
    ISBN 9781541541962 (eb pdf) | ISBN 9781541540330 (lb : alk. paper) |
    ISBN 9781541545496 (pb : alk. paper)
Subjects: | CYAC: Dating (Social customs)—Fiction. | High schools—Fiction. |
    Schools—Ficti on.
Classification: LCC PZ7.1.R82 (ebook) | LCC PZ7.1.R82 Dat 2019 (print) |
    DDC [Fic]—dc23

LC record available at https://lccn.loc.gov/2018027162

Manufactured in the United States of America
1-45238-36620-9/17/2018

TO J.W.

« «

1

"*Marvelous* meat loaf?" Jenae read the day's lunch special from the sign above the cafeteria entrance. Her tone made it clear she gave the meal zero chance of living up to its name. "It's the last day of school. They could at least serve pizza!"

Maribel shrugged. It didn't matter what was on the menu. She couldn't eat. Her stomach was a fluttery mess. She couldn't even think straight. When she was younger, the approach of summer vacation filled her with excitement. This year was different. Rather than anticipating the fun-filled, homework-free days of summer, she was *dreading* the end of the school year.

It was all because of Evan. She'd rather go to school year-round than wait two whole months to see him again.

After paying for their food, they carried their trays to a table where their friends Nic, Aaron, and Annalise were already sitting.

"You're going tonight, right?" Annalise asked both girls, her voice squealy with excitement.

Jenae nodded vigorously, but before Maribel could answer, Aaron chimed in. "Of course they're going. They put so much work into this party."

As co-captains of the school's environmental club, Maribel and Jenae had organized a beach cleanup the previous weekend. Along with a handful of other volunteers, they'd picked up nearly twenty pounds of litter from Casker's Cove, the site of tonight's beach bonfire. The event—celebrating the end of the school year—was going to be epic. Still, Maribel bit her lip and wrinkled her nose.

"I'm not sure," she said.

Her friends turned and stared at her. Aaron's eyes widened in surprise. "Are you kidding, Mari? You cleaned every last candy wrapper and bottle cap off the beach so it would be perfect for the party."

"That's not the only reason," she couldn't help pointing out. "We want to keep trash off the beach, so it won't pollute the lake and kill the fish and other marine life."

"Yeah, yeah, we know." Nic pushed his glasses farther up on his nose. "You two want the whole world to hug the trees, kiss the fishes, and all that jazz. But let's get real. You have to go to the bonfire. *Everyone's* going to be there."

Without thinking, Mari turned and scanned the cafeteria. She spied Evan sitting with his friends at a table in the corner. She wondered if *he* would be at the bonfire.

"Yeah." Mari turned back to the group. "And everyone's going to have a date. Except me."

Jenae flashed a sheepish grin in Aaron's direction. The pair had started dating only recently, while Nic and Annalise had been a couple for most of the school year.

"You'll hang with us," Jenae told Mari.

Mari knew Jenae and the others would make sure she didn't feel like a fifth wheel. Still, it would be better to have a date. Her eyes sought out Evan once again. She couldn't help it. She'd spent months staring at him from across classrooms and cafeterias. She had tried to keep her crush a secret, but her friends caught on long ago.

"Evan's an idiot if he doesn't want to go out with you," Annalise said, and the others nodded in agreement.

Mari shrugged one shoulder. "I don't think I'm on his radar. Even though I put myself in his path whenever possible." She blushed when she thought of all the times she hovered at the water fountain near his locker so that she could "accidentally" cross paths with him when he approached. "I'm invisible to him."

"You know . . ." Annalise leaned forward. "Girls don't have to wait for guys to do the asking."

The rest of the group echoed Annalise's comment. "Yeah," Nic said. "We don't live in medieval times."

"I know, but—" Mari hesitated. The thought of asking Evan to the party turned the fluttering in her stomach into a total tsunami. "What if I ask him out and he says no?"

"He won't." Jenae rested a hand on her friend's shoulder. "And if he does, well, at least you'll have two months to get over it before school starts again."

"I guess you're right." Mari watched as Evan lifted a piece of not-so-marvelous meat loaf to his mouth. His marvelous mouth. A mouth she'd imagined kissing a million times.

She looked back at her friends. They all flashed encouraging smiles in her direction. Aaron gave her two thumbs-up. He was the newest member of the group, and Mari didn't know him as well as the others. But he was fun to be around, and Jenae said he was a good boyfriend. Seeing the two together made Mari a little envious, though she was happy for her friend.

"Go for it," Aaron said.

Mari looked over her shoulder again. Evan had already finished his lunch and was exiting the cafeteria. She turned back to her friends. Then, gripping the edge of the cafeteria table for support, she announced, "Okay. I'll do it."

2

After lunch, on the way to class, Mari took her usual detour through the science wing, past Evan's locker—number 718. She glanced around casually but didn't see him nearby.

She drifted over to the water fountain— her usual stall tactic when looking for Evan. Then she stopped short, remembering what day it was. Her school was notorious for end-of-year pranks. Last year, someone had rigged the water fountain so that water shot straight up into the face of whoever pressed the button. Selina Miller got blasted so badly that her makeup ran down her face in streaks that made her look like a sad clown.

It was hilarious and heartbreaking at the same time.

Though the pranksters probably wouldn't repeat the same gag two years in a row, Mari didn't want to take that chance. Instead she pretended to be interested in a handmade poster advertising the end-of-year bonfire party. She felt silly staring at the poster as though she was learning about the event for the very first time. But now that she'd decided to ask Evan out, she didn't want to back down. And she'd rather do it here in the hallway than during math—their only mutual class. The hallway was bustling with activity, which meant probably no one would pay attention to her and Evan. And if things went badly, well, at least there were plenty of exits nearby.

She'd been staring at the poster for a long time, and there was still no sign of Evan. Just as she was about to give up, she heard his name. It was spoken in a high-pitched tone by one of two girls who were approaching the water fountain. Funny how Evan's name seemed to float above the hubbub in the hallway and zing its way straight into her eardrums. It was like some part of her consciousness was constantly scanning the atmosphere for evidence of his existence.

"Are you sure he's going?" the shorter girl asked.

"He told Troy he'd see him there." The other girl swept her long blonde hair to one side before bending to drink. Apparently, the water fountain hadn't been sabotaged after all. The taller girl stood and wiped her mouth with the back of her hand. "I picked out the perfect top. It's red with a scoop neck and peekaboo sleeves. But I can't decide between my black jeans or a tulle skirt."

Mari ambled over to the water fountain. She stood behind the two girls, waiting her turn.

"Chill, Chelsea," the short girl said before stepping up to the fountain. "Whatever you wear, you'll be the hottest thing at the bonfire."

The tall girl, Chelsea, let out an exaggerated sigh. "Besides Evan."

Mari felt a sudden, suffocating tightness in her chest. If someone like Chelsea was

interested in Evan, did Mari even stand
a chance?

As Chelsea was stepping away from the
fountain, she sneezed.

Mari said, "Bless you," and reached into her
backpack, feeling around for a pack of tissues.
"I've got tissues if you want one."

Chelsea waved her hand dismissively. "Um,
no thanks." The girls continued down the hall,
their voices fading.

Mari took her turn at the fountain, guzzling
slowly. Finally, she couldn't wait any longer.
She had to get to P.E. class.

She took one last glance over her shoulder.
There he was. Evan. Standing at his locker. It
was the perfect time for Mari to make a move.
If she had the nerve.

"It's now or never," Mari whispered to
herself. Striding toward locker 718, she called
out, "Evan."

He looked up. She took a step closer
and was about to speak when Aaron, Jenae's
new boyfriend, appeared at her side. "Hiya,"
he said, giving her a playful punch on the

shoulder. Mari shot him a death glare and he blushed, suddenly realizing he'd interrupted *the* moment. "Later," he said. Then he turned away and reached for the combination lock on his own locker.

"Yeah?" Evan asked. His eyes met Mari's, and the corners of his mouth lifted slightly. That small hint of a smile gave her the courage to continue.

"I, um, I was wondering if—" she began.

The rest of her words were drowned out by a thunderous noise as dozens—no *hundreds*—of golf balls tumbled out of Aaron's locker. They hit the floor and bounced in all directions. Aaron went wide-eyed with shock; he clearly hadn't known that someone had filled his locker with golf balls. Someone yelled, "Pranked!" and Evan doubled over in laughter.

Mari was too stunned to speak. Besides, Evan's attention was no longer on her. Like everyone else, he was distracted by the golf balls pouring from Aaron's locker down the hallways. He said something, but Mari couldn't hear his words over the shouts and laughter filling the halls. Teachers and students came out of nearby classrooms to see what had caused the commotion. Some kids grabbed on to each other to keep from tripping.

The warning bell rang, and the crowd began to scatter. Mari stepped forward and the world seemed to suddenly tilt on its axis. She realized too late that her foot had landed on a golf ball. She fell backward, landing on her butt in the middle of the hallway.

3

Mari didn't know which hurt more—her tailbone or her pride. Kids were crowded around, laughing at her. Her cheeks flamed with embarrassment. The worst part was that this had happened right in front of Evan!

She glanced around, then frowned in confusion. Evan had been standing there a moment ago, but now he was nowhere in sight. He must have rushed off to his next class. Chelsea was among the students who lingered in the hall.

Before today, she'd barely known who Chelsea was. They had no classes together and no mutual friends. But now that she knew that they both liked Evan, she could only think of Chelsea as a rival. So it was extra annoying to see her standing there laughing at Mari's expense.

In that moment, Mari decided not to be a victim. She refused to let Chelsea and the others see that their laughter bothered her. So she joined in. "It's a great day for public humiliation," she said, a fake smile plastered on her face.

Last year, Mari had been part of the crowd that witnessed Selina Miller drinking from the booby-trapped water fountain. Now she regretted laughing at Selina.

"You okay?" someone asked.

Mari looked up to see Aaron standing over her, hand outstretched. She took his hand and pulled herself up. "I'm fine." Actually, her shoulder was beginning to throb. She had a vague memory of banging it against the wall as she went down. But she said, "Thank you." Then she hurried toward the gym, careful not to step on any more golf balls along the way.

* * *

Twenty minutes later, Mari was back in the science wing, but now it looked like a crime scene. A line of orange cones blocked the hallway. A school security officer had been posted at the entrance.

The P.E. teacher had assigned Mari and two other students to gather all the golf balls. The prankster, whoever he or she was, had unintentionally donated to the school's collection of athletic supplies.

Mari held up a pair of empty mesh bags and told the guard, "Ms. McAllister sent us to pick up the golf balls."

The officer nodded and let them through the temporary blockade. "Check inside the classrooms and bathrooms too. They could have rolled anywhere."

Mari noticed that there were several other people in the hallway. The school nurse and the vice principal crouched over Mr. Motoyama, a science teacher. Mr. M sat with his back against the wall, an ice pack pressed to his forehead. A bloody handkerchief was on the ground next to him.

Mari felt terrible. She liked Mr. M. He peppered his lectures with corny jokes. They weren't very funny, but the way he chuckled at his own puns was endearing.

"What happened?" she asked as they cautiously approached.

"He slipped on a golf ball and hit his head on a locker door," the vice principal explained. "He'll probably need stitches. Whoever did this is going to be in serious trouble. Did any of you see what happened?"

"I did," said Mari. "The golf balls came out of Aaron Daniel's locker, but he seemed totally shocked when it happened. I don't think he had anything to do with it."

The vice principal nodded. "He claims he's innocent. He's in the principal's office now. We'll get to the bottom of it."

The three girls divided the task of rounding up golf balls. Mari volunteered to check the classrooms and restrooms in the science wing while Diane and Anjelia worked their way down opposite sides of the hallway. They'd only been given two mesh bags, which Mari handed to Diane and Anjelia since most of the balls were pooled in the hall.

Mari still had her backpack with her and figured she could use it to carry the golf balls she gathered. Unzipping the backpack, she entered the first classroom.

Crouching low, she looked under desks and behind wastebaskets, collecting more than a dozen golf balls and plopping them into her backpack.

Even though the boys' bathroom was empty, she felt weird as she tiptoed inside to pluck a golf ball from underneath the sink. This one glittered under the fluorescent lights. Holding it closer she saw it was imprinted with a logo in gold ink. It had faded, so she couldn't tell what it was supposed to be. Some kind of bird, perhaps.

She noticed the same faded logo on some of the other balls. As she worked, she wondered how someone could have filled Aaron's locker with golf balls without his knowledge. He *had* truly seemed surprised, but she supposed it could have been an act. For Jenae's sake, she hoped that Aaron was innocent.

When the period was almost over, the girls met up in the hall. Mr. Motoyama and the nurse were gone. The vice principal was watching the janitor clean the area where the science teacher fell. Always squeamish, Mari averted her eyes in case there were still any signs of blood.

"We must have more than a hundred golf balls here," Anjelia said. She held up her bag. "I found thirty-seven. I wonder how Aaron got them all into his locker." With a sideways glance at Mari, she added, "Or, you know, whoever did it."

Mari shrugged one shoulder, feeling a stab of pain as she did so. "We should get back to P.E."

The vice principal turned toward the girls. "Is it true you were injured too?" he asked Mari.

She shook her head. "I fell, but I'm okay. It was no big deal."

"Good to hear, but I still want you to get checked out by the school nurse." He turned to Diana and Anjelia. "You two get back to class."

Diana promised to let the coach know Mari

had been delayed, then she and Anjelia hurried toward the gymnasium.

The vice principal's cell phone buzzed. He glanced at the screen, then told Mari, "After you've been checked out by the nurse, stop by Admin. There's an incident report you'll need to sign. I have to go talk to the cops."

The *cops*?

Mari's head was spinning. Why were the police involved? It was a simple school prank. Whoever was responsible didn't intend for anyone to get hurt. Now she *really* hoped that Jenae's boyfriend was not to blame.

4

Mari couldn't lift her left arm above her head without wincing in pain. The school nurse gave her an ibuprofen and put the arm in a sling.

"Looks like a mild sprain," the nurse told her. "If the pain continues for more than a day, have your parents take you to your family doctor."

At the Admin office, she read the incident report the vice principal had written. It included a list of names—students who had witnessed the incident. She saw her own name and Aaron's, along with a few others she recognized. But not Evan's.

"Can you think of anyone else who was in the hallway at that time?" the administrative assistant asked her.

"Why?" Mari asked. "Just because someone was there doesn't mean they had anything to do with it."

"Of course not," the administrator agreed. "We just want to talk to everyone who may have seen anything. Now, think back. Do you remember anyone in particular?"

The truth was, when she pictured the scene, the only face that came into focus was Evan's. She remembered his slight smile as he gazed at her. A split second later, a gazillion golf balls exploded in front of her eyes—and the question that had been on the tip of her tongue instantly evaporated.

Her mouth went dry at the memory. The first time in her life she tried to ask a boy out on a date, and it was a total disaster! She squeezed her eyes shut and shook her head, hoping to erase the event from her memory.

She opened her eyes again. Evan had nothing to do with the prank, so it shouldn't matter if she gave them his name. Still, he might not appreciate being called down to the principal's office on the last day of school. And Mari would die if Evan found out that *she* was the one who reported his presence at the scene.

"No," she said, as sincerely as she could manage. "No, I don't."

* * *

The rest of the afternoon passed in a blur. Teachers rarely lectured on the last day of school. Instead, kids signed each other's yearbooks and chatted about their summer plans.

Mari's last period was math, a class she shared with Evan and Jenae. The teacher had put two challenge questions on the board, offering candy to whoever solved them first. A few of the straight-A kids were scribbling away, but Mari's mind was not on math. She gazed at Evan, whose desk was diagonal to hers, and let out a soft sigh. She wondered whether they'd have any classes together next year.

Jenae leaned over and said in a hushed tone, "Ask him."

Mari wrinkled her nose. She'd blown her earlier attempt at asking Evan out. She didn't think she had the nerve to try again. She turned to Jenae and mouthed "No."

Jenae pointed up at the clock on the wall. The minutes were ticking down. It was now or never.

The bell rang, and students sprang to their feet. Mari moved slowly, still sore from her earlier injury. As she lifted her backpack onto her right shoulder, Jenae darted past. She whispered in Mari's ear, "Do it!"

Evan was still at his desk, putting his things back into his backpack. As Mari watched from the corner of her eye, she noticed something small and colorful fall to the floor. Evan zipped up his backpack, slung it over one shoulder, and headed to the door.

Mari crouched down and retrieved the colorful object from the floor. It was a harmonica-shaped keychain with green and yellow wooden pegs poking through each side. Glad for the excuse to speak to Evan, she caught up to him by the classroom door. Just as he was about to exit, she tapped him on the shoulder.

He turned and flashed her a wide smile.

5

"I dropped this," Mari said, holding the keychain toward Evan. "Err, I mean, *you* dropped it. I picked it up." She pointed back at his desk. "Over there." *Stop talking*, she told herself, but her mouth kept moving. "I saw it fall out of your backpack, and um, figured you'd probably need it."

As he reached out to take it, his fingertips brushed against hers briefly. The sensation was electrifying.

"Yeah, I do. Thanks." He pocketed the keychain and looked back at her, still smiling.

This was the moment she'd been waiting for. She had Evan's attention, and there were no golf balls raining down on them. A few kids lingered by the door, but the classroom was mostly empty. She'd never get a better chance to ask him to the bonfire. But when she opened her mouth to speak, all she could manage to say was, "You're welcome." She felt her heat rise and imagined color creeping into her cheeks. She hated the fact that her face turned bright red whenever she was nervous.

His smile faded. "You all right?"

She nodded quickly. "Fine. Why?" The words came out sharp and defensive. Not the tone she intended at all.

Evan took a step back. "You fell down. After lunch?" His gaze fell to the sling that held her left arm in place across her chest. "I heard you were sent to the nurse's office."

"Oh, that. Yeah, it was no big deal." The fact that he was curious about her condition gave Mari hope. Maybe, just maybe, he cared about her. Before she could explore that thought further, someone shouted Evan's name from the hall. She looked over his shoulder and saw a few of his friends. One of them hooked

his arm through the doorway and called,
"Come on!"

Evan gave Mari a quick nod, and then he
was gone. Along with Mari's hopes for a date
to the beach bonfire.

* * *

Mari flopped facedown on her bed and let out
a long sigh. It was almost 7:00 p.m. Most of
her classmates would be at Casker's Cove by
now, enjoying the bonfire. Jenae had urged
her to go, but she just couldn't. Not after her
embarrassing exchange with Evan in math
class. She was bummed, but there was no way
she could face him after that.

Instead she'd decided to stay home for a
boring night with her parents. After dinner
they'd started watching an alien movie Mari
had seen a half dozen times before. After a
little while, she grew bored and went upstairs
to her bedroom.

"You okay?" her father had asked as
she trudged up the stairs. "Is your arm
bothering you?"

Over dinner she'd explained what happened and insisted she felt fine. She didn't even need the sling any longer. But now, it seemed like a convenient excuse to get out of family time. She rubbed her shoulder. "It hurts. I think I'll lie down."

Now, she rolled onto her back and stared up at the ceiling. She fished her phone out of her back pocket and opened a gaming app. Anything to take her mind off the bonfire.

But it was no use. She'd spent weeks looking forward to the bonfire, and now she was missing out.

After a few minutes she gave up on the game. She paced her room, looking for a distraction.

The sundress she'd originally planned to wear to the bonfire was still hanging on the back of her bedroom door. Another reminder of her dashed hopes for a date with Evan. Though it was clean, she grabbed it off the hanger and tossed it into the laundry bin.

Just then her phone pinged. She picked it up and glanced at the screen. Jenae had texted her.

Bonfire is epic! You should come! Evan is sad
and ALL ALONE.

So what if he's alone, Mari thought. Did she really need to embarrass herself in front of him again? Twice in one day was plenty.

She was starting to type out a reply when a photo popped up on her screen. It showed several teens—including Aaron, Nic, and Annalise—sitting in a semicircle at a fire pit, with their backs to the lake. Some held marshmallows on sticks. Aaron was playing the guitar. Annalise leaned against Nic, a dreamy smile on her face. At the edge of the group, Mari saw Evan, sitting by himself. She zoomed in on his face, trying to read his expression. Not sad exactly, but he didn't look like a guy enjoying an epic party.

Ping!

Another text from Jenae.

Hurry! Bet he won't be lonely for long . . .

《 6

The sun was setting by the time Mari arrived at the beach. Once she made up her mind to go, she'd dashed about her room, getting ready in record time. Her dress was slightly wrinkled from being shoved in the hamper, but she wore it anyway. She smoothed out the creases with her hands as she got out of her mom's minivan.

"Thanks for driving me, Mom," she said.

"You're sure your arm is feeling all right?" her mom asked skeptically.

"Yeah, it just ached a little earlier, but it's fine now," Mari insisted. "And I promise I won't stay out too late."

After watching the minivan pull away from

the parking lot, Mari made her way toward the beach. She saw the flickering glow of flames near the south end of the cove and headed in that direction. As she grew closer she heard laughter and music.

Aaron was playing a tune on his guitar. Several kids sang along. As Mari reached the party, she scanned the faces of the crowd. She didn't see Evan anywhere. Jenae was stretched out on a beach blanket with a cooler full of soft drinks next to her.

Their eyes met and Jenae waved at Mari. "Over here! I saved you a spot on my blanket."

Mari dropped her backpack onto the sand and sat cross-legged next to her friend. Then she reached into the cooler for a can of soda.

Annalise elbowed Nic. "Look who's here!"

Nic reached over with his soda bottle, clinking it with Mari's. "Cheers!" He pointed to a picnic table nearby. Trays were loaded with graham crackers, chocolate bars, and marshmallows. "Go make a s'more," he said.

"In a little while," Mari said. Her eyes scanned the crowd for Evan. She thought she was being casual about it, but as usual, her friends could tell what was on her mind.

Annalise spoke up. "He's around here somewhere."

"Who?" Mari said, her tone innocent.

Nic answered, "Evan, of course." The others exchanged knowing glances.

Jenae leaned over to Mari and whispered, "I saw him walking along the beach a few minutes ago." She pointed down the shoreline. "He went that way."

Mari nodded, her excitement growing. If she caught up to him on the shore, away from the crowd, it would be easier to talk. "How do I look?" she asked her best friend.

"Great." Jenae flashed a thumbs-up and whispered in her ear, "Go get him!"

* * *

Mari walked briskly down the beach, slipping her sandals off when she reached the shore. She liked the feel of sand between her toes and cool water gently lapping over her feet. Her heart skipped a beat when she caught a glimpse of

Evan silhouetted against the setting sun. He was so good-looking, it was hard to believe he didn't have a girlfriend.

Maybe that would change tonight.

She slowed her pace as she grew nearer. She didn't want him to think she was chasing him. Her mind raced as she tried to think of something clever to say when they met. As the noise of the bonfire party receded, she heard a voice. Evan's.

Then, a high-pitched giggle. Definitely not Evan.

Trees dotted the shore along this part of the lake, obscuring her view. Mari took cover behind a large palm and peered around it. Her heart thudded in her chest.

Evan was standing on the shore with Chelsea—the girl who'd laughed when Mari slipped on the golf balls that morning. They were both facing the lake, tossing small objects. *Skipping stones*, Mari realized. Chelsea didn't seem to be very good at it. She let out another laugh when her rock failed to make any ripples on the water's surface.

Mari's chest tightened. She could barely breathe. Was this really happening? She felt foolish hiding behind the tree, but she was frozen to the spot. Afraid to make a sound and attract their attention, she stood and watched the scene play out in front of her.

Why hadn't Jenae told her that Chelsea was with Evan? *She must not have known*, Mari reassured herself. Her best friend would never have sent her down the beach if she knew Evan was with another girl.

It wasn't Jenae's fault. Chelsea clearly had a crush on Evan and had probably made her move the moment he set out on a walk by himself. Could she blame the girl? That was exactly what Mari had hoped to do.

Mari looked up at the darkening sky and wondered, *What if?* What if she'd asked Evan out that morning? Before the golf ball prank, or during math class? Or what if she'd arrived at the party earlier? Would she be standing in Chelsea's place? She'd certainly had her chance. More than one. But she'd blown it.

She blinked and refocused on the two of

them. She wished she could hear what they were saying but didn't dare move closer. Holding her breath, she strained to make out their words.

Then, silence.

Standing perfectly still in the shadow of the tree, Mari watched Evan loop his arm around Chelsea's waist and pull her in for a kiss.

‹‹

7

Mari spun on her heels and took off running
down the beach. The sand between her toes
no longer felt inviting. The water was cold,
and the soles of her feet scraped against
the rocky shore. Too late, she realized she
was no longer holding her sandals. She
must have dropped them somewhere along
the way.

She didn't dare turn back. All she wanted
now was to go home.

Stars filled the night sky. As a kid, she'd
made countless wishes upon those stars. Most
never came true, but the instinct was still
there. She focused on a particularly bright star

and thought to herself, *I wish I could go back in time. Before this awful day even started!*

She kept running, not slowing until she reached the edge of the bonfire party. She was out of breath, heart pounding wildly.

Jenae was standing near the fire pit, a roasting stick in her outstretched hand. The marshmallow on its tip was golden brown.

"Jen—" Mari sputtered as she tried to speak. She couldn't catch her breath.

Jenae's eyes widened when she saw Mari. "What's wrong? Did you find Ev—"

Mari grabbed her friend by the arm and pulled her from the fire. "Shhh! I don't want *everyone* to know."

When they were a few yards from the crowd, Mari let go of Jenae's arm.

Jenae looked at the tip of her roasting stick. It was empty. "Aww, you made me lose my marshmallow."

In that moment, Mari was furious. Jenae cared more about a stupid marshmallow than about her best friend. It was her fault Mari was even here. If Jenae hadn't texted her about

Evan, saying he was lonely, she never would have come.

"I thought you said he was alone," Mari said sharply. "But he's not. He's with Chelsea!"

"Chelsea Littman?" Jenae wrinkled her nose in distaste. "I didn't even know she was here. But they're not together, are they? Maybe they're just friends."

"He *kissed* her!"

"Aw, don't cry," Jenae said.

Mari's eyes were watery, and her chest was heaving from the run. But she wasn't crying. At least, she hadn't been. She looked at the kids circling the fire pit. They seemed mellow, carefree. Enjoying a warm night with friends and good music. She caught a few of them staring in her direction. She knew she must look terrible.

"I'm not . . . *crying*!" A few more heads turned in her direction. Then the music stopped. Aaron had set his guitar down and was walking toward them. All eyes on her, Mari felt humiliated.

Jenae stepped closer to Mari. She reached

out to put her free arm around her friend's shoulder.

Mari pushed her away. "It's all your fault. You told me to ask him out today, and I fell on my butt. Then you got me to rush down here. And once again, I end up looking like a total idiot!"

"I just wanted you to have a good time." Now Jenae looked like *she* was on the verge of tears. "It's not my fault you don't have a boyfriend!"

Aaron stepped between the two girls and asked, "What's going on?" When neither answered, he turned to Jenae and said, "Let's get back to the party."

Jenae looked like she wanted to say something. But then she took Aaron's hand and turned her back to Mari, strolling back to the fire pit.

8

Mari was glad to see her father's pickup truck pull into the beach parking area. Her mother would have asked a million questions about the party. She would have noticed that Mari looked like she'd been crying. Mari didn't feel like talking about it.

Her father noticed only one thing. "Where are your shoes, Maribel?" he asked her when she climbed barefoot into the truck's passenger seat.

"I don't know," she admitted. "I took them off to walk along the shore. Then I couldn't find them."

Her father let out a bark of laughter. "That's

pretty ironic. You and your club cleaned up every scrap of trash off the beach. Then you left your shoes behind. What if they end up in the lake?"

Mari groaned. "I'll go back tomorrow and look for them," she promised. "It will be easier to see in the daylight."

Her father nodded his approval, and they drove the rest of the way home in silence.

When they reached the house, the living room was empty. The alien movie was paused on the TV screen. The smell of buttered popcorn filled the air.

"Back so soon?" her mother called from the kitchen. "Why don't you join us? I'm making popcorn."

Mari bypassed the kitchen on her way to the stairs. "No, thanks. I'm super tired."

"Wait." Her mother emerged from the kitchen carrying a big plastic bowl. "I want to hear about the bonfire."

Mari yawned dramatically as she headed up the stairs. "I'll tell you all about it in the morning. Good night."

* * *

Up in her room, Mari lay on her bed and stared at her phone. She scrolled through her social media feeds, looking at photos of the bonfire. Her mood worsened with each picture. She'd worked so hard to prepare for the party and she'd basically missed the entire thing.

She swiped her screen again and her heart stopped. A classmate had just uploaded a group photo from the party. In it, Evan was sitting by the fire pit, Chelsea at his side. His arm was draped around her shoulder. She was smiling, her face lit by the fire. They looked perfect together but all wrong at the same time.

Mari closed her eyes and imagined herself in Chelsea's place. The warmth of the fire on her face, the sound of her friends' laughter. The feel of Evan's arm around her. She opened her eyes again and stared at the photo. *Why her? Why not me?* she wondered.

She logged off and set the phone facedown on her nightstand. It was too late for what ifs. She had to move on. She'd force herself to get over Evan. At least she had two whole months before she'd have to face him again. She just hoped that by the time school began again, everyone would have forgotten about her meltdown at the party.

She reached into the drawer of her nightstand and pulled out her journal. She'd been writing in it since the beginning of the school year.

She flipped back through it. Evan's name popped up on page after page.

She'd been such a fool.

She tore the page from the journal and crumpled it up. She tossed it across the room and watched it bounce off a wall. It felt good, so she ripped another page out.

Before long, she'd torn twenty pages out of the journal.

Suddenly, her phone pinged. She knew it was another text from Jenae. On the ride home from the beach, she'd received several texts from her best friend, wanting to know if she was okay. She'd ignored them all. She was still angry at Jenae for encouraging her to go to the party.

She flipped off her light and turned on her

side. Lying in the darkness, she tried to think of anything but Evan.

Her phone pinged again. Jenae could be so persistent. It was one of the things she'd liked about her. Jenae didn't give up. She worked harder than anyone to achieve her goals. It had been Mari's idea to start the environmental club at school. But when she couldn't convince her science teacher to approve it, Jenae stepped in. She was the one who got Mr. Motoyama and the administration to allow the club.

Remembering Jenae's commitment to the cause, Mari softened. It wasn't Jenae's fault Evan was with Chelsea instead of her. A knot formed in her stomach. She owed Jenae an apology.

She sat up in bed and reached for her phone. Leaning against the headboard, she read the notifications on the illuminated screen.

She had several texts and one missed call from Jenae. But the most recent message wasn't from Jenae or any of her other friends.

It was from an unknown number.

Would you like a do-over?

Mari frowned at her phone. The text made no sense. Who had sent it and what did they mean by a "do-over"?

For a breathless moment, she considered the possibility that the text was from Evan. But no, he was probably still snuggling with Chelsea on the beach. He didn't even have her number.

Another ping and a new message from the unknown number popped up on her screen.

This is a limited time offer. Rewind the day.
Make a different choice. Reply YES or NO.

She remembered her wish to go back in time to before this day even started. If only such a thing was possible.

Rewind the day? She thought about what would have happened if she'd made a different choice that morning. If she'd asked Evan to the bonfire and gone to the party as his date. They would have listened to music together and laughed with their friends. They would have strolled hand in hand down the shore and skipped stones on the lake. They would have held hands, maybe even kissed . . .

The texts had to be a joke, but she couldn't figure out who'd sent them. And the same instinct that had her wishing on stars made her feel a twinge of excitement as she reread the messages.

Rewind the day. Make a different choice.

Could it be true?

No, of course not.

Yet . . . fingers trembling slightly, she typed YES and hit SEND.

9

Mari didn't know how long she slept. It seemed like only minutes could have passed since she drifted off before a knock on her door roused her. She turned onto her stomach and tried to fall back asleep. She was exhausted. Dark thoughts and weird dreams had kept her tossing and turning through the night.

Her mother knocked again, calling through the closed door. "Maribel, are you up? You need to dress for school. Hurry!"

Mari groaned. *Dress for school? Has Mom gone crazy?* It was Saturday, and school was out for summer. *And what time is it, anyway?*

She reached for her phone on the nightstand.

Her fingers instead found her journal. She flinched, remembering how she'd torn the pages out in misery.

She pulled the book closer to her and blinked. Its pages were intact. Rubbing sleep from her eyes, she sat up straighter and looked again. She flipped through the journal. Her eyes landed on the pages mentioning Evan.

How can this be? She clearly recalled ripping them to smithereens. *Had it been a dream?*

Her mind flashed to the last thing she remembered. The weird texts she received the night before. She reached for her phone.

The mysterious texts from the unknown number were gone. Other messages were missing too. The ones from Jenae checking to see if she was okay. And the one Jenae sent earlier, telling her to hurry to the bonfire because Evan was alone. In fact, the last text in her in-box was from Thursday night.

Her sundress was hanging on the back of her bedroom door. It showed no signs of being worn the night before. It was possible her mother had come into her room and hung it up during the night. But what about the sandals she'd lost on the beach? She threw her bedcovers aside and rushed to the closet. She flung the door open and gasped. There sat her favorite sandals.

"Maribel!" Her mother's tone was growing harsher. "Breakfast. Now!"

* * *

In the dining room, Mari's mother was pouring coffee into two mugs. She slid one across the table to Mari's father, who was watching the morning news channel on the TV. Mari sank into the chair across from him and stared at the TV. Her eyes lasered in on the date running across the bottom of the screen. *Yesterday's* date.

It couldn't be.

"Is this today's news?" she asked her father as she reached for a box of cereal.

Still staring at the TV, he said, "Yup."

Mari's mother poured milk into her own bowl and then passed the carton to Mari. "That's a funny question."

"I *feel* funny," Mari said. "Like I'm somehow on the wrong timeline."

Her father turned to her and laughed. "You've been watching too much sci-fi."

"I didn't even watch the alien movie last night," Mari said. "That was you two."

Her mother tilted her head, eyeing Mari curiously. "What alien movie? We were salsa dancing last night."

Her parents had enrolled in a Thursday night salsa class a few weeks ago.

Her father took a sip from his coffee mug and then said, "I wouldn't mind watching an alien flick tonight, though. What do you ladies say?"

Mari's eyes flicked from one parent to the other. She scanned their faces for signs they were messing with her. Her dad enjoyed a good prank and could often coax her mom into participating.

But she saw no hint of the devilish twinkle he usually got in his eyes when he was fooling around. Her skin prickled. She felt light-headed. Like the world was somehow off-kilter. Nothing made sense.

Her mother took a sip of her coffee, then gave a small nod. "Sounds good to me. But Mari's going to the beach tonight."

"The beach?" her father asked. "Why?"

"The bonfire," her mother replied. "She's been planning it for weeks!"

He nodded. "Right, right. Last day of school."

In that moment, confusion gave way to certainty. Mari knew it must be true. Weird as it was, the text had been for real. She'd been granted a do-over. She gulped a few spoonfuls of cereal and shot up from her chair. As she dashed up the stairs, she called over her shoulder, "I have to hurry, or I'll be late for school."

Her mother shouted after her, "That's what I've been telling you!"

10

It was a major case of déjà vu. The morning was exactly the way she remembered it. Kids were dressed the same as they'd been the day before. They said all the same things.

When Jenae scrunched her nose and read the menu board at lunch, Mari knew she was going to say, "*Marvelous* meat loaf? It's the last day of school. They could at least serve pizza!"

As usual, they sat with Nic, Aaron, and Annalise. As they discussed the bonfire, Mari predicted every word uttered by her friends. When Nic teased her for wanting the world to hug trees and kiss fishes, Mari knew that was her cue. She turned and looked at the precise spot she knew Evan would be sitting. The sight of him made her palms instantly sweat.

"You have to go to the bonfire," Nic was saying for the second time. "*Everyone's* going to be there."

"Yeah. And everyone's going to have a date. Except me."

Once again, her friends encouraged her to ask Evan out, and once again, Mari agreed to do it.

But this time was different.

This time she really *would*.

She'd been given a second chance—and she wasn't going to let it slip through her fingers.

* * *

After lunch, Mari headed to Evan's locker. It didn't surprise her one bit that he wasn't there. She found herself glancing up at Aaron's locker, number 721. She bit her lip and looked around. She was the only person in these halls who knew what was inside that locker. *No*, she silently corrected herself, *someone else knew. The person responsible for the dangerous prank.*

Remembering her fall, she reached up to rub her left shoulder. She almost laughed as she realized it didn't hurt. Of course it didn't—she hadn't injured it yet! She lifted the shoulder up and down, telling herself to enjoy the pain-free range of motion while it lasted.

She walked over to the poster advertising the bonfire. As she stared up at it, she thought about second chances. Did her do-over just apply to asking Evan out? Could she change other parts of the day? Could she maybe *not* fall on her butt and make a huge fool of herself?

Just then she saw Chelsea and her friend walking down the hallway. They approached the drinking fountain.

Last time, Mari had stood in line behind them and eavesdropped on their conversation. Now she knew what they would say. And she wanted to experiment.

She hurried toward the fountain, reaching it just before the two girls. She bent and took a long, slow drink. Behind her, Chelsea told her friend about the outfit she'd chosen for the party. This time, Mari had a picture-perfect image in her mind of the red blouse with the scoop neck and peekaboo sleeves.

This time, when the shorter girl told Chelsea to "chill," they were still waiting for their turn at the fountain. Mari delayed, taking as long as she could. Finally, she straightened. Instead of walking away, she turned to Chelsea and said, "Bless you."

One second later, Chelsea sneezed.

As Mari continued down the hall, she heard Chelsea's friend say, "That was weird." She kept walking, wanting to be out of the danger zone when the balls tumbled out of Aaron's locker. A short distance away, she leaned against a wall as though waiting for a friend. Her eyes scanned the crowd. She was looking for Evan, but if anyone asked she'd say she was meeting up with Jenae.

Finally, she saw Evan approach.

A thrill went through Mari. Like she was watching a movie, anticipating a jump scare. In her mind, the soundtrack was speeding up. This time, she was at a safe enough distance to enjoy the show.

She watched Evan put in the combination on his lock and swing open the locker door. There was a slight hint of a smile on his lips.

Mari's insides quivered. She remembered poor Mr. Motoyama being tended to after his injury. Suddenly she wondered, *Should I have tried to stop the prank?* But there was no time. Aaron had nearly reached his locker. Mari couldn't prevent it from happening, so she settled for trying to spot anyone looking guilty or suspicious in the crowd.

Evan turned then, jolting Mari back to the present. He was looking at Aaron, who'd just reached up to his own locker. He'd probably said, "Hi, dude," or another Aaron-like greeting.

Then the avalanche of golf balls rushed from Aaron's locker. They hit the floor and bounced in all directions. Mari watched Aaron closely this time. He really did look surprised. His mouth fell open and his eyes were wide.

Someone yelled, "Pranked!" and Evan doubled over in laughter.

Mari watched as Chelsea teetered and

tried to right herself. Then she fell backward, landing on her butt in the middle of the hallway.

Kids pointed and laughed. She couldn't help but laugh too—and then instantly felt ashamed. She wasn't behaving any better than Chelsea and her friend had when their roles were reversed.

Chelsea's face turned a bright red. Her friend reached down to help her up.

The warning bell rang, and Mari started toward the gym.

"Hurry up, Maribel," a voice called as she rounded the corner. "Or you'll be late for class."

"I will." She cast a glance over her shoulder and saw Mr. Motoyama, the science teacher, emerging from a classroom.

Mari's stomach lurched at the memory of the teacher leaning against the wall with a bloody rag in his hand. He'd needed stitches for a deep gash on his forehead.

If she didn't act quickly, history would soon repeat itself.

11

Mari spun on one heel and hurried after the science teacher. "Mr. M, wait!"

He slowed his pace but kept walking. "What is it?" he asked with a glance over one shoulder.

"Look out!" She was nearly out of breath when she caught up to him. "Golf balls. Everywhere. Don't trip!"

They turned the corner, and the teacher looked around. "I see what you mean."

The final bell rang. She'd be late for P.E. again, but she didn't mind. She'd saved Mr. Motoyama from a serious injury.

"Thank you for the warning. If I had

slipped on a golf ball, I would have been teed off." The teacher chuckled at his own joke. "Get it? Ha!"

Mari smiled at the corny joke. "I've got to run."

She wasn't surprised when the girls' P.E. coach sent her and two other students to round up golf balls in the science wing. Backpack still slung over one shoulder, she walked back to the science wing with Diana and Anjelia.

Once again, a security officer stood in front of a line of orange cones.

Once they'd gotten past the guard, Mari noticed the school nurse and the vice principal crouched over a third person. *Who?* She'd saved Mr. Motoyama.

As she neared, she got a better view of the injured person. Her heart lurched. It was Jenae! She sat with her back against the wall, an ice pack pressed to her forehead. The sickening sight was made even worse because Mari felt responsible.

"What happened?" she asked as they cautiously approached.

The vice principal said that Jenae had slipped on a golf ball and hit her forehead against a locker door. She would probably need stitches.

Mari covered her mouth with one hand. She felt as though she was going to be ill.

"Whoever did this is going to be in serious trouble," the vice principal added. "Did any of you see anything?"

Mari admitted that she'd witnessed the prank but insisted that Aaron couldn't have been the one who planned it. Mari handed the mesh bags to Diana and Anjelia to started collecting golf balls, figuring she would use her backpack again. She knelt next to Jenae. The nurse was applying a bandage to her forehead.

"Is she going to be okay?" Mari asked.

The nurse nodded, then told Jenae, "An ambulance is on the way. You're going to be checked out at the hospital."

When the nurse left them to go speak to the vice principal, Jenae looked up at Mari. Her eyes were red from crying. "Do you think I'll have a scar?"

Mari didn't know, but she said, "No. Probably not." She patted her friend's leg reassuringly. "I'm so, so sorry."

"Why are *you* sorry? You didn't do it."

Mari hesitated. "I just feel like . . . maybe I could have done something differently. I could have stopped you from getting hurt."

"That's ridiculous." Jenae grabbed Mari by the hand. "You really don't think Aaron did it? If he did, I . . . I don't know what I'd do."

Mari felt even worse. Not only had Jenae been injured, but she feared her own boyfriend might be to blame.

"It wasn't him," Mari insisted. "I'm sure."

"But who else would have been able to get the golf balls into his locker? They'd have to know his combination."

Mari shrugged. "I don't know," she said truthfully.

* * *

By the time the three girls had retrieved all the wayward golf balls, paramedics had arrived for Jenae. The vice principal was watching the janitor clean the area. Mari averted her eyes, not wanting to see her friend's blood.

"We must have more than a hundred golf balls here," Anjelia said, holding up her mesh bag. "I found thirty-seven. I wonder how Aaron got them all into his locker. Or, you know, whoever did it."

"It wasn't him," Mari insisted again. "We should get back to P.E."

The vice principal strode toward the girls. "Come with me," he told Mari. "We're taking statements from anyone who witnessed the prank." Turning to Diana and Anjelia, he added, "You two get back to class."

The vice principal's cell phone buzzed. Mari knew the message alerted him that the police had arrived on campus. "Stop by Admin to give your statement. I have to go talk to the cops."

Mari nodded. She wondered what the police would do about the prank. And if Aaron wasn't responsible, who was?

* * *

The rest of the afternoon was like a sitcom rerun. Things happened just like the first time. Kids signed each other's yearbooks and chatted about their summer plans.

But in math class, Jenae was missing. By now everyone had heard that she'd been taken to the hospital. Their teacher reported that Jenae was getting stitches but would be fine.

Mari kept her eye on the clock. The minutes were ticking down on the last day of school.

Finally, the bell rang. Jenae wasn't there to tell her to "go for it," but that was all right. Mari had spent the entire day preparing for this moment.

As students sprang to their feet and raced toward the door, she hung back. She waited for Evan's keychain to fall to the floor, then she moved closer. She bent to retrieve the harmonica-shaped keychain. As she examined the colorful pegs that poked through each side, she thought of Mr. Motoyama's joke. *If I'd slipped on a golf ball, I'd have been teed off. Get it?*

That's what these wooden pegs are, she realized. *Golf tees.* The keychain was a golf tee holder.

She turned it over in her hand. "SWANSEA" was printed in gold letters on the other side.

Evan had already zipped his backpack and was headed for the exit. Mari hurried to catch up to him. She called his name and tapped his shoulder. He turned and flashed a familiar smile.

"You dropped this." She held the keychain toward him. "I saw it fall out of your backpack and figured you'd need it." She didn't stumble over her words this time. She'd practiced them a dozen times in her head.

He reached out to take the keychain. Once again, Mari felt a spark when his fingertips brushed against hers.

"Yeah, I do. Thanks." He pocketed the keys and looked back at her, still smiling.

"You're welcome." She returned his smile. She had butterflies in her stomach, but she wouldn't let them take over. *You got this*, she told herself. She opened her mouth, but he spoke first.

"Sorry your friend got hurt earlier," he said, his smile fading.

"Yeah. Me too."

Someone shouted Evan's name. His friends from the cafeteria were waiting in the hall. One of them hooked his arm through the doorway and called, "Come on!"

Evan started to turn away, but Mari said, "Wait!"

She steadied her nerves and smiled. "Will you be my date to the bonfire?"

12

Only a few seconds could have passed between Mari's question and Evan's answer, but it felt like forever. Finally, he gave a slight nod.

"Yeah, sure."

The words set off fireworks in her brain. She had a date for the bonfire. The date of her dreams! She couldn't wait to tell Jenae and the others.

Evan was looking at her expectantly. She realized it was her turn to speak. But her mind was blank. She hadn't practiced this part! All day she'd known just what to say and do. But from this moment forward, everything would be different.

This was when her do-over truly began. She couldn't mess it up.

"Cool," she said at last. "Pick me up?"

"Nah, can't." He ran his hand over his hair and shook his head. "I've got to work after school. I'll meet you at the beach."

Evan gave her a wink, then turned and headed out the door.

Mari said, "See you at the party" to his back.

* * *

"Let me guess," Mari said to her father when she came down the stairs. "Spaghetti and meatballs."

The table was set for dinner, but the food was still in the kitchen. Out of view from the dining room.

"Good guess. The aroma is obviously pasta sauce. But how did you know it was spaghetti?"

Mari shrugged. Scoring a date with Evan had put her in a playful mood. She was having fun "predicting" her parents' actions.

"I must be psychic," she said now. "Bet I know which movie you guys are going to watch tonight."

Mari's mother entered the room carrying a large bowl of spaghetti. "We haven't decided."

"I think you should watch *Martians at the Mini Mall*."

Her dad nodded. "Funny, I was just thinking about that movie. Too bad you won't be home to see it with us."

Mari ate quickly and refused her mother's offer of seconds. "There's going to be lots of food at the bonfire," she explained.

Mari raced upstairs to change and get ready for the party. She took her time getting her hair and makeup just right. Her favorite sundress was hanging on the back of her bedroom door. She reached for it but changed her mind. The dress was now associated with some unpleasant memories. She could picture herself running down the beach in that dress, barefoot and crying.

Instead, she chose an emerald green top that brought out the color of her eyes. She paired it with black jeans and the same sandals she'd worn before. They really were her favorites. And the pretty green and gold beads on the sandal straps matched her blouse. This time, she vowed to keep them on her feet.

An hour later, her mother dropped her off at Casker's Cove. Music and laughter mingled with the sound of waves gently lapping the shore. A couple dozen teens were gathered around the fire pit, some holding roasting sticks up to the flames. She recognized several of her friends. She knew Jenae wouldn't be among them. She'd texted earlier to say she was home from the hospital but didn't feel up to a party. She'd also sent a photo of her forehead with the caption: "Seven stiches!" Mari still felt responsible for her friend's injury, though she'd never be able to explain why.

Aaron was sitting on a folding chair, playing his guitar. Annalise was on a blanket, leaning back against Nic. Mari waved to them, her eyes still scanning the crowd for Evan. She finally spotted him, sitting off to one side. Their eyes met, and he smiled and waved her over.

"Saved you a seat," he said, moving a large duffel bag off the chair next to his. "I came straight from work on the bus, so I still have my school stuff." He gestured at her backpack, which she'd just lowered to the ground. "What's your excuse?"

Mari rolled her eyes. "My mom packed me snacks and water—even though I told her there'd be food and drinks. And she insisted I bring a hoodie in case I get chilly." Mari didn't mention the sunscreen and first aid kit her mother had also shoved into her backpack at the last minute "just in case."

Evan took a sip of his cola. "She's one of those helicopter moms?"

"Not really. But she probably circled the parking lot a few times to make sure I didn't get kidnapped on my way over to the fire pit."

Evan chuckled softly, then put an arm around her shoulders. "Well, you're safe with me now."

They pulled their chairs closer to the fire to roast marshmallows. Evan let the flames lick his marshmallow, burning its surface to a crisp. "The best way," he insisted, laughing. Mari held hers above smoldering embers until it turned golden brown. Then she blew on it to cool it off.

"Ouch!" she said when she bit into the molten goo. "Hot, hot, hot!" Evan laughed again.

The crowd swelled as more kids joined the party. Chelsea had arrived shortly after Mari. Her arm was in a sling. Mari felt a little sorry for her. Not because of the sling. The shoulder injury was probably just like hers had been. A minor sprain. Nothing serious.

But she saw how Chelsea kept glancing over at her at Evan. She knew what the girl was probably feeling. She'd felt the same way when their roles were reversed.

When they finished their snacks, Evan stood. The setting sun cast shadows across the lake. He held a hand out toward Mari. "Want to go for a walk along the shore?"

Mari remembered the lakeside kiss between Evan and Chelsea. The scene was burned into her memory. But it was about to change. She reached out and took Evan's hand.

◀◀

13

The evening sky looked as though it had been painted by an artist's brush. *Magical*, Mari thought. Her gaze took in the sky as she walked hand in hand with Evan.

They were approaching a small stand of trees. Mari recognized the large palm tree she'd hid behind last time. Her heart sped up. Soon, she knew, she'd get to kiss Evan.

She slowed her pace. She wanted to savor every second. But also, she wanted to get to know Evan. They'd been in the same math class all year but had barely spoken. She knew nothing about his life outside of school.

"Do you have any brothers or sisters?"
she asked.

He nodded. "An older sister and a younger
brother."

She smiled. An only child herself, she'd
always wanted siblings. One of each seemed
like the perfect number. "What are their names?"

"Emily and Sean."

"What about pets?" she continued, figuring
that learning more about Evan would make her
feel closer to him.

"Um, no." He let go of her hand and bent
to pick up a stone. Then he walked to the
water's edge and looked out at the lake. "Used
to have a dog, but he died a few years ago."

"What was his name?"

"Luke. As in Skywalker."

"You're a *Star Wars* fan." Mari smiled, glad
to know they had this in common.

With a quick flick of his wrist, he sent the
stone in his hand rocketing toward the water.
It skipped across the surface once, twice, then
sank. Frowning, he said, "My brother named
the dog. He's the *Star Wars* nerd."

"Oh." Mari leaned against a tree. "What kind of movies do you like?"

"Pretty much anything off the beaten track. Indie films, documentaries. I don't like superheroes or space aliens."

"Me either," she lied.

As they talked, she watched him skip three more stones. The first two were duds, sinking as soon as they struck the water. He palmed the third one and rubbed its surface with his thumb. "Nice and flat. This is the one."

This is the one, Mari repeated in her head. But she wasn't thinking about a rock.

"Woo-hoo!" Evan shouted as his stone flitted across the water. "One, two, three, four, five. Personal best!"

She flashed him a wide smile.

She had more questions for him. She wanted to know how he spent his weekends, what video games he liked, what was on his playlist. Did he play sports? Was he planning to go to college? But for now, she'd keep those questions to herself.

They stood side by side, looking out at

the lake. Then Mari picked up a small pebble. She'd never been good at skipping stones, but she'd thrown lots of coins into fountains. So, after making a silent wish, she tossed the pebble high into the air.

The sky had grown dark. She couldn't see where the pebble hit the water, but she heard a tiny plunk. She wondered if her wish would come true. It was almost time to find out.

She turned to look at Evan. He stared back at her.

They stood in silence for a moment.

"I keep asking about you," she said finally. "Do you have any questions for me?"

He took a step closer to Mari, then looped an arm around her waist. "Just one," he said as he pulled her close. Then, he asked, "May I kiss you?"

Not trusting her voice, she simply nodded.

14

As they kissed, it seemed like the rest of the world melted away. Mari imagined the night stars swirling around the two of them. No one else existed.

Mari had spent a million math classes picturing this. But it was even better than she imagined.

After a few perfect moments, Mari took a step back and breathed in the night air.

Evan's face was handsome in the moonlight. He slipped his fingers through hers. Grinning, he guided her farther down the shore.

Mari was quiet as they walked. The kiss was replaying on an endless loop in her brain.

When the silence became awkward, she went back to questioning him about his life.

It turned out they watched some of the same TV shows and had similar tastes in music. His part-time job kept him too busy for video games or sports.

"Where do you work?" she asked.

"Swansea." Evan pointed toward the opposite shore.

Mari squinted into the darkness. The name sounded familiar, but she couldn't place it.

"The golf club," he said. "On the other side of the lake."

Then she remembered where she'd seen the name. "Your keychain. The one you dropped at school. It's from there?"

He fished the keychain from his pocket and nodded. "My work keys. I owe you big time. They'd dock my pay if I lost another set. This one," he said, wriggling a small silver key, "is for one of the staff golf carts. It costs a fortune to re-key those carts. If a key gets lost, my boss freaks out. He's afraid someone will find the keys and come steal the cart."

"Work keys," Mari repeated slowly. "And those wooden things are golf tees. At first I thought they were game pieces, like where you move pegs on a board until there's one left."

"Yeah, we sell those games in the club shop. Along with keychains and other souvenirs. Golfers buy all sorts of stuff made out of golf tees or golf balls."

Her throat went dry at the mention of golf balls. She pictured a river of golf balls spilling out of Aaron's locker. Golf balls she'd spent an entire class period retrieving from the science wing. She remembered seeing a logo on some of the balls. Faded, but recognizable as a bird. Not just any bird, she realized now. A swan.

Mari felt dizzy. She closed her eyes. A whirlpool of emotions swirled inside her, not all of them good.

Then Evan put his arms around her. She hadn't realized she'd gotten cold until that moment. It was a nice feeling. She wanted more moments like these. She wanted, more than anything, to be Evan's girlfriend.

So what if he worked at the golf club? That

didn't mean he was the one who planted the balls in Aaron's locker.

Eyes still closed, Mari tried to recall the moments just before the prank. She remembered both versions of the events. The first time, she'd just called Evan's name. She was gathering up the courage to ask him out. He'd said, "Yeah?" and turned toward her. There was a slight smile on his face. She'd believed he was smiling at her.

But after the do-over, things were different. Mari had watched from a distance. She'd seen Evan glance over at Aaron as he opened his locker. They exchanged a few words. Evan had the same hint of a smile on his face. Like the mischievous expression her father got when he was up to something.

Evan's locker was close to Aaron's. It would have been easy for him to look over Aaron's shoulder and see the combination. He probably stored the golf balls in his own locker. Then, when no one was around, he transferred them to Aaron's. She remembered seeing him leave the cafeteria early.

And another strange thing. Both times, Evan disappeared immediately after the prank. Like he didn't want to be observed at the scene.

She opened her eyes and stepped back. "The golf balls that were stuffed into Aaron's locker? I saw a logo on them. A gold swan. Could they have come from your club?"

She expected him to deny it. She *hoped* he would deny it. Instead, he nodded.

"Of course they did. I'm the one who put them there." He tipped his head back and laughed. "Did you see Aaron's face? Greatest. Prank. Ever!"

15

"You have to tell them." Mari took another step back. Hands on her hips, she stared at Evan. She couldn't believe he was laughing. Sure, it was a prank. But someone had gotten hurt. Her best friend.

He stopped laughing. "*Tell them?* You're kidding, right?"

"No. They're trying to figure out who did it. The cops were there. I had to give a statement. They asked me to name everyone who was in the hall when it happened."

"The cops?" Evan's face paled. "Did you tell them I was there?"

"No." At the time, she had no idea Evan

was involved. She'd just wanted to spare him from being called to the principal's office. Now she felt a stab of guilt for not being honest. "But *you* should. It's serious. Jenae slipped and fell. She had to get seven stiches! And Mr. Motoyama—" Mari stopped short. She realized that in this version of reality, the science teacher hadn't been injured.

"What about him? Did he fall too?"

"No," Mari recovered quickly. "But his classroom is near Aaron's locker. And he's old and he's nice. It would have been awful if he got hurt." She felt her eyes moisten. She looked away, not wanting Evan to see her cry.

Evan noticed how upset she was. He pulled her close again and spoke softly. "It was a prank. Like last year. Remember Selina Miller and the water fountain?"

She inhaled sharply. "Did you do that too?"

"No! It was a couple of seniors. I just wanted to carry on the tradition. I promise, I didn't mean for anyone to get hurt. *Especially* your friend."

Mari stood in his embrace. She could feel

his heart beating against hers. She believed him. He didn't plan the prank with the intention of harming anyone. "I know," she said on a sigh.

He pulled back and looked her in the eye. "You can't tell anyone, Mari. I mean it. If I get in trouble, I could lose my job. I could lose *everything*."

"I'm sure they'll understand."

Evan's tone grew sharp. "No, they won't. I'm on probation at work. Nothing big. I forgot to punch out a few times, and I lost some keys. I'm a good worker. One of the best. But if they found out I took all those balls—"

"Wait. You *stole* the golf balls?"

"No, not really. The club 'retires' old, worn-out golf balls. They go into a huge bin. We donate them to the YMCA or other programs. We're allowed to give a bucketful to pretty much anyone who asks. So I donated some to myself."

She nodded. That didn't sound so bad. "Still, I have to tell Jenae."

Evan took her hand. He guided her over to a grassy spot. They sat side by side, looking out at the lake. "It's not just the job I'll lose. The club gives scholarships to employees. My application was already approved. I just have to keep up a B average and keep working there senior year. My parents need that money to help pay for my college, Mari."

Mari took it all in. She didn't know what to say. Telling the truth was the right thing to do. But she didn't want Evan to get in trouble with the school or his job. And the cops were involved too. What if Evan got into trouble with the law?

Evan leaned back onto his arms. Gazing up at the night sky, he said, "You ever wish on a star when you were little?"

She nodded and stared up at the stars. "Seems like just yesterday."

"Your wish ever come true?"

"Once."

He let out a sigh. "Well, I wish I could take back the stupid prank. But I can't. I know that. So I just want to pretend it never happened. Don't tell anyone, Mari. Please. Promise me."

She turned to face him. She could tell by

his expression he was truly worried. His future was on the line, after all. She felt silly for making a big deal out of it. After all, it was just a prank.

"I promise."

⋏ ⋏ ⋏

They walked back toward the south end of the cove to rejoin the others.

As they got closer to the group, Mari stopped. Something on the shore had caught her eye. "Someone left a soda bottle on the beach."

Evan let go of her hand and strode to the water. She smiled, glad that he shared her interest in keeping the lakefront clean. But before she could say so, he turned and hurled the bottle toward the lake. It went high in an arc and then splashed a good distance from shore.

Mari gasped. "Why did you do that?"

Evan smiled, apparently pleased with the shot. "Why not?"

"I was going to recycle that bottle. Now it's at the bottom of the lake!" She told him about the environmental club she'd formed with Jenae. "Last weekend we cleaned tons of trash off this very beach. Including a bunch of golf balls, by the way."

"Yeah, I bet. Some of the guys at the club like to hit them into the lake."

She shot him a death glare. "They do?"

"All the time. Those 'retired' balls I told you about? A lot of them end up in the lake. The guys call it a 'burial at sea.'"

Mari frowned. The lake bed must be littered with thousands of golf balls. She didn't want to think about the fish living among all that garbage. "Do you do that? Hit golf balls into the water?"

Evan shook his head. "I don't even like to play golf."

"But you threw that bottle . . ."

"Glass won't hurt anything. People throw bottles into the ocean all the time, right? They even put messages inside. Eventually it all turns into sea glass. And isn't glass made from sand, after all? So it's all cool."

"It's *not* cool, Evan. That bottle will take

a million years to break down. It doesn't belong there!"

He expelled a sigh of frustration. "Okay, I'm sorry. I won't do it again."

"Really?"

Evan drew an X over his chest. "Cross my heart."

Mari nodded, relieved. They continued walking. Then she said, "We have to stop the golf club from polluting the lake."

"Whoa, what?" Evan held a hand up in protest. "They're a bunch of rich golfers. They won't listen to us. They do what they want. My job is to help them do it."

And you're good at it, Mari thought ruefully. *One of the best.*

They were nearing the fire pit now. Heads turned their way as they approached. Evan lowered his voice. "Hey, let's not argue in front of everyone."

He reached for her hand and led her back to the chairs they'd abandoned earlier.

Aaron looked up from his guitar and gave Mari a wink. He knew she'd been crushing on

Evan for months. He seemed glad to see them together at last.

She was glad, too, but she felt unsettled. It wasn't just the prank. Talking to Evan didn't come as naturally as she'd thought it would. It was forced and awkward. Not at all how she'd imagined. *This is just a first date*, she reminded herself. She was holding hands with the guy of her dreams. And she was surrounded by her friends—well, most of them, anyway.

She still had a lot to learn about Evan. And he still knew practically nothing about her. But they'd have plenty of time to build a relationship.

In the meantime, she'd try to relax and enjoy the evening.

16

When Evan went to get them more drinks, Mari glanced at her phone. She'd missed a text from Jenae.

How's the bonfire?

Mari looked over at Aaron. His guitar was resting on his lap. He was leaning back, taking a break between songs. He looked a little lost.

She'd been foolish to ever think Aaron might have pulled the prank. He wasn't that kind of guy. When Mari fell on her butt, it was Aaron—*not Evan*—who helped her up. Jenae was lucky to have him for a boyfriend.

Mari lifted her phone and snapped a photo of him. She sent the picture to Jenae with the message:

Not the same without you! Aaron is sad and all alone.

A few seconds later, another text from Jenae.

Poor guy. And how is the date?

Mari typed "perfect," and was about to hit send. Then she deleted the word and began again.

Almost perfect.

She looked at the time before sliding the phone back into her pocket. It was getting late. Some kids, including Nic and Annalise, had already left. The temperature was dropping. Mari shivered as she leaned toward the fire.

"You okay?" Evan handed her a Coke. "You've got goosebumps on your arms."

"It is chilly." Mari pulled her backpack onto her lap. She unzipped it and reached inside for her hoodie. As she tugged the hoodie out of the bag, a bunch of golf balls came tumbling out with it. She'd forgotten they were still in there. After signing the incident report, she'd gone straight to her next class. She'd never made it back to the gym.

She was leaning forward to pick them up when she heard a shrill voice.

"What are you doing with those?" Chelsea was standing in front of Mari. Arm still in a sling. Expression even more sour than before. With her free hand, she bent and picked a golf ball off the ground. "You did it," she said, loud enough for everyone to hear. "You're the one who booby-trapped that locker!"

"What?" Aaron shook his head. "No way. Not Mari."

"I did not! That's crazy," Mari responded.

Chelsea's friend was standing now. "She was acting really weird today. Like she knew something was going to happen."

Chelsea nodded. "That's right. And she

was hanging around forever. Waiting. She kept staring at Aaron's locker."

That part is true, Mari thought. But she couldn't explain how she knew about the prank before it occurred.

The other kids were staring at her now. One boy told her to turn herself into the police. "Your friend had to go to the hospital. You're gonna be in big trouble."

"I got hurt too," Chelsea said, wiggling her arm in the sling for emphasis.

"Did you frame me?" Aaron narrowed his eyes at Mari. "The principal grilled me for over an hour."

"No!" Mari shook her head forcefully. "I . . . I didn't—" Choking back tears, she couldn't finish her sentence. Seeing the look in Aaron's eyes really hurt her feelings. *Does he really believe Chelsea's accusations?* she wondered.

Someone shouted, "The vice principal said whoever did it could be expelled!"

This was getting out of hand. Why didn't anyone believe her?

She looked around. Diana and Anjelia

could back up her story. But she didn't see either of them.

There was only one person at the party who knew Mari was innocent.

She turned and looked at Evan. He held her gaze for a moment, then looked down at his feet. He said nothing.

Mari knew he was in a difficult position. If he admitted being the prankster, he'd be in big trouble. With the school, his job, his parents, and maybe even the police. He had a lot to lose by telling the truth. And only one thing to gain.

Mari looked beyond him to the stars twinkling over the lake. She wished that Evan had thought she was worth the risk.

17

Mari brushed tears out of her eyes as she headed to the parking lot. An evening that had started out as magical had turned miserable. She wished she'd never accepted the do-over.

Her father picked her up to bring her home. As usual, he didn't ask many questions. Nor did he notice she'd been crying. She was grateful for that. How could she explain how badly she'd messed things up? As they drove, she got a text from Jenae:

Aaron told me YOU put the golf balls in his locker. How could you? I'm going to have a scar on my forehead for the rest of my life!

Mari quickly responded.

It's a lie. I can explain. Call you tomorrow.

Jenae's reply was instant:

Is that why you kept apologizing for my
accident? Because YOU DID IT?!

Mari felt helpless. She typed out the only
response she could think of.

I didn't! I swear.

A few minutes later Jenae replied.

Then WHO DID?

Mari had hesitated. She hadn't ratted Evan
out at the bonfire, and she wouldn't now. She
didn't want him to lose his job or his scholarship.
More important, she wouldn't go back on her
word just because he turned out to be a jerk.
Mari slowly typed out:

I can't tell you. I'm so sorry.

She tucked her phone back into her pocket. It didn't ping again for the rest of the drive.

Back home in her room, Mari lay on her bed and stared up at her bedroom ceiling. Her thoughts were a jumbled mess. She needed to calm down. She wouldn't be expelled, she told herself. The coach and the vice principal would confirm that she only had those golf balls in her backpack because she'd been cleaning up.

But what about Jenae? She'd never forgive her for keeping the prankster's identity a secret. And she couldn't tell her about the do-over. She couldn't tell anyone about that. Even her best friend. They'd think she was lying.

The worst part was realizing how foolish she'd been. All those months, she'd dreamed about dating Evan. She'd built him up in her mind. The perfect guy. But he wasn't. At least not for her. She wanted someone who shared some of her interests, who cared about the environment. Most of all, she wanted someone who would have her back.

She picked up her phone and opened a social media app. Several kids had posted photos of the bonfire. She flipped through them until she saw one of her with Evan, earlier in the evening. Evan's arm was draped around her shoulder. She was smiling, her face lit by the fire. At the time, she thought they were perfect together. Now she knew she'd been wrong.

The more she looked at the picture, the worse she felt. It was just like the photo of Evan and Chelsea from her original reality—before the do-over. Evan's expression was the same as she remembered. He looked just as pleased to be on a date with Mari as he had been with Chelsea. Mari felt completely replaceable.

She scrolled down. The photo had thirteen comments. The first was from Chelsea.

Glad you had fun at the bonfire while some of us suffered from your prank earlier.

Several of her classmates expressed their surprise. A few kids she didn't know chimed in, calling Mari names.

Mari was humiliated. Being shamed on social media was even worse than falling in the hallway at school.

Only Nic, who'd left the party early, seemed to doubt the story. He left a comment that simply read:

I don't believe it.

That was encouraging, Mari thought. Her heart sank when she reached the last message in the chain. It was from Evan.

Saw it with my own eyes. It's always the quiet ones.

That stung. Apparently, Evan was more interested in protecting his reputation than standing up for Mari. She blinked back fresh tears.

More posts were being added to the thread, but Mari couldn't take any more. She was about to shut down her phone when it pinged. A text message from the unknown number.

Would you like to Un-Do your Do-Over?

Another ping, another message.

Reply YES to go back to your original reality.

She still didn't know who or *what* was behind these weird texts. But this time, she didn't hesitate before typing her reply:

YES.

* * *

The sun was high in the sky by the time Mari woke the next morning. She reached for her phone to check the time. As she did so, she felt a stab of pain in her shoulder. Did that mean . . .?

Sitting up in bed, she tested her shoulder further. *Ouch.* Yep, definitely sprained.

Her nightstand was covered with torn bits of paper. The pages she'd ripped from her journal.

Another good sign.

She checked her phone. The mysterious do-over texts were gone. Instead she had a string of messages from Jenae, asking if she was okay. The last text read:

> Please don't be mad at me. I didn't know
> Evan would hook up with Chelsea. What
> a loser!

She didn't know who Jenae was calling a loser, Evan or Chelsea. But either way, Mari appreciated her friend's sympathy.

Mari scrolled through Jenae's messages again, looking for the "Seven stiches" photo. But it didn't exist. Her friend had never been injured. Relief flooded her body.

She checked her social media feeds. Everything was back to the way it was before. Including the photo of Evan and Chelsea, seated together at the bonfire.

The do-over had truly been undone.

As she continued scrolling, she saw a post from Chelsea that had a bunch of likes and comments.

Found out at the bonfire tonight that EVAN was
the golf ball prankster!! He actually admitted it
to me, thinking it was funny . . . Can't believe
I wanted to date him! What a jerk. Considering
turning him in to administration . . .

Mari laughed aloud and clicked the "like"
button. She knew exactly how Chelsea felt.
*Maybe Chelsea isn't so bad after all. To be honest,
she didn't act any worse than I did. Evan clearly
fooled us both.*

Although she felt bad about Evan dealing
with the consequences, she would have felt
even worse if Aaron was blamed for a prank he
didn't do. Chelsea's post had cleared Aaron's
name, and Mari had kept her promise of not
reporting Evan.

She still remembered everything about her
date with Evan. How excited she'd been that
everything she'd hoped for had worked out.
But now she knew that the guy she'd built up in
her head wasn't so great after all. This summer,
she planned to make the most of her time
with her real friends. And maybe once school

started in the fall, she'd be able to look at Evan without thinking about how awful their date had been.

She reread Jenae's message, ashamed that she'd ever blamed her best friend for anything that happened. She typed a response:

It's not your fault. I probably dodged a bullet anyway. I have a feeling Evan isn't the right guy for me.

Moments later, her phone pinged, and she read Jenae's response.

You're probably right. Wanna hang out later?

They made plans to catch an afternoon movie, then Mari rolled onto her side and stared out the window. The sun was shining brightly, but she was in no hurry to get out of bed. School was out for summer.

And she was happy.

ABOUT THE AUTHOR

BRENDA SCOTT ROYCE is a writer and editor with more than a dozen books to her name. She won grand prize in the 2015 Writer's Digest Annual Writing Competition. When not writing, she enjoys hiking and spending time in nature. She lives outside Los Angeles with her son and two rescue cats, Morty and Mabel.